HIDE!

Steve Henry

I Like to Read®

HOLIDAY HOUSE • NEW YORK

Mike naps.

Pat sees a fish.

Pat sees more fish.

Pat sees more and more.

The fish have fun.

A shark!

Pat can't hide.

Pat still can't hide.

Pat needs help.

The shark has Pat.

Pat is safe.

Now Mike has fun.

But Mike needs help.

He can't go up.

The fish help Mike.

Pat and Mike are safe.